Fabulous!

Sensational!

Award winning!

Unforgettable!

A masterpiece!

Tired of those old advertising adjectives?
You'll be relieved to know that *not one* applies to

Madvertising

(or, Up Madison Avenue)

More **MAD** Humor from SIGNET

Madvertising
or
Up Madison Avenue

**Written
by DICK DE BARTOLO**

**Illustrated
by BOB CLARKE**

**Edited
by NICK MEGLIN**

A SIGNET BOOK from
NEW AMERICAN LIBRARY
TIMES MIRROR

New York and Scarborough, Ontario
The New English Library Limited, London

SIGNET TRADEMARK REG. U.S. PAT. OFF. AND FOREIGN COUNTRIES
REGISTERED TRADEMARK—MARCA REGISTRADA
HECHO EN CHICAGO, U.S.A.

SIGNET, SIGNET CLASSICS, MENTOR, PLUME AND MERIDIAN BOOKS
are published *in the United States* by
The New American Library, Inc.,
1301 Avenue of the Americas, New York, New York 10019,
in Canada by The New American Library of Canada Limited,
81 Mack Avenue, Scarborough, Ontario M1L 1M8,
in the United Kingdom by The New English Library Limited,
Barnard's Inn, Holborn, London, E.C. 1, England.

FIRST SIGNET PRINTING, JULY, 1972

7 8 9 10 11 12 13 14 15

PRINTED IN THE UNITED STATES OF AMERICA

FOREWORD

How This Book Came To Be...

First, before I get into the actual reason why I wrote this book, I want to say that you are an unusual reader. Unusual because you are reading the *foreword!* A recent survey showed that 97% of all book readers do *not* read the forewords; and out of the remaining 3% who *do* read it, 97% don't read the *book!* That leaves approximately .3456% who read *both* the foreword and the book, and that is who this particular foreword is aimed at. Actually, I think it would be easier for those 2.7 people to telephone me at home and I'll personally explain to them how this book came to be, but then that would leave these 3 pages blank—just the sort of short-changing this book is fighting against!

Simply stated, this book is dedicated to deception in advertising. Not *for*, stupid, *against!* The fact that I am an author doesn't make things any different at the cash register. I spend $40 a week on food, in the vicinity of $90 when I need a new suit, and about $20 for shoes. This is right in line with the cross-section of American shoppers. And yet, as a typical average shopper, I sometimes feel that I'm being taken advantage of. Like yesterday. I was purchasing an elephant when the thought occurred to me—how do I know this elephant is really fresh? Maybe it's yesterday's elephant! Maybe elephant is *always* 39¢ a pound and not the special "marked down from 49¢" as the sign said! Store managers, I have learned, are not beyond putting the new elephants in the back and the old up front! I've heard of cases where they actually *changed the dates* on the elephants! One store sold elephants at 29¢ a pound, but further investigation turned up the fact that tusks and trunk were "optional extras!" Stores in high income areas sold the very same elephants as "pachyderms" at 89¢ a pound! It now becomes obvious why a book such as this is necessary to the consumer! Of course, no book would be truly effective without top-notch art work and layouts, but rather than spring for the money a top-notch designer would cost, I settled instead for Bob Clarke. He agreed to take on the assignment for 50% of what the publisher was paying me. I thought that was a very fair arrangement, especially since I told him I was getting 50% less than I really was, which means he was actually getting 50% of 50%! My research on deceptive figure practices was already paying off! Now if Bob Clarke doesn't read forewords, I've got it made!

A great book must always have a great editor. But here again, what is a great book? Certainly not this one! This is a hack book! So it was only natural that I thought of Nick Meglin when the subject of editors came up. Here again a deceptive advertising ploy worked—I convinced Meglin this book was a *public service*—so he did the job free!

Now you too, dear foreword reader, can benefit from my research and study! Just continue reading *after* the foreword, and I can save you thousands of dollars each year with little hints and insights like . . .

1. If you buy a structure over 30 stories tall, make sure the price includes wrapping! I recently bought a 52 story building and the clerk charged me $56,000 extra for brown paper and string!

2. Shop around! Don't jump at the first price tag you see! A housewife friend of mine saw an atomic reactor for $250,000. Not heeding my advice, she bought it. On the way home she saw the *same* atomic reactor in another store window for only $220,000! Unfortunately, she had paid cash for the first one, so she was out the extra $30,000. This kind of money can add up!

3. Don't shell out more than you have to. Recently I bought a World War II tank which was delivered to me at my sixth floor walk-up apartment in Manhattan. The driver mumbled and grumbled and put on a big show how difficult it was for him to get it up the steps, but since I had already paid $40,000 for the tank I certainly didn't think I should have to cough up another quarter for a tip! I just ignored his obvious "sweat and strain" performance, signed the receipt, and saved myself 25 cents! The dentist bill resulting from his punching me in the mouth, however, came to $450, so even after reading this book you'll still have to use a certain amount of judgement!

Dick De Bartolo

When the world came into being, so did one of the basic principles of advertising...

...tell them they can't have it, and they'll want it!

And when man learned how to communicate, he learned another principle of advertising . . .

**Translation:
reduced from four
oxen in trade, to
two oxen, one goat!*

EVERYBODY LIKES TO THINK THEY'RE GETTING A BARGAIN!

"Never give them the best first..."

Some other principles...

"Never use two words..."

**'When you can use many
that mean the same thing"**

CONTAINS ONE FULL
GOVERNMENT ACCEPTED
FIRST QUALITY
SIXTEEN OUNCE POUND

Be sure to put the same product in as many different size packages as possible...

CORN FLAKES Single Serving

CORN FLAKES

FOR TWO

CORN FLAKES

FOR FOUR

FAMILY SIZE CORN FLAKES

This Envelope Contains One Single **CORN FLAKE**

Make *everything* you do to the product,
good or bad, into something "NEW!"

NEW! **DIFFERENT!!**

SPECIAL PACKAGE!!!

UNLIKE THE OLD KLEENIX*

KLEENIX

*contains fewer tissues than ever before for the same amount of money!

Take the old standard items:

and merchandise them new ways:

Now take up half the room on your table... use only half the motion of your arm... with the modern new product........

MORON'S SALT 'N' PEPPER ALL IN ONE SHAKER

when it rains... she gets wet!

Create new uses for the same old product, no matter how far out...

RICE KRIPSIES
MAKES A GREAT BURGLAR ALARM!

Rice Kripsies

Spread Rice Kripsies under each window and near each door...anyone entering will alert you with a crunching sound!

MOVING?

VAN

PACK YOUR EXPENSIVE DISHES AND GLASSWARE IN:

RICE KRIPSIES

GOING TO A WEDDING?

Throw RICE KRIPSIES
instead of rice...
distinguish yourself
from the rest of the crowd!

MOTHS EATING YOUR CLOTHES?

Spray Rice Kripsies white and put
them in your closets... Nearsighted
moths will think they're mothballs!

When you've got a warehouse full of an item that no longer sells, like hula-hoops, find a new market for them, like:

Only a square would use a square picture frame, but a Jet-Setter like you should insist on the

ALL NEW

GIANT CIRCULAR PHOTO FRAMER

in rustproof plastic and decorator colors

only $6.95

Now, for the first time you can own

LUNA-HOOPS

circular in shape, just like
our space capsules

made of space-age
PLASTIC

they orbit your waist!

only $7⁹⁵

26

Another often used advertising ploy is to mention huge, outrageous sums of money in an ad, so when they get to their "bargain price," which is usually the list price, it seems ridiculously low. Add to that the so-called "free merchandise" you'll get when you fulfill certain requirements and you have the typical record club ad that looks something like this...

27

GIANT SAVINGS
FROM THE LIFELONG RECORD CLUB!

Do you know how much it would cost
to bring the entire cast of
NO NO NANETTE
into your home to perform the original score?
Depending on where you live, it would cost between
$56,987. and $123,876.

But Now, for only **$6.95**, about 1/200 of that price,
the fantastic LIFELONG RECORD CLUB enables you to have
that very same cast perform for you whenever you want...
that's almost a 2345% saving!

But that's not all...

If you join the

LIFELONG
RECORD CLUB

TODAY!

You can get in on this

SPECIAL DEAL!

Simply buy NO NO NANETTE and just five other records now, and agree to buy five more records each month for a period of five years for each of five members of your family, at a saving of up to 5%, then you will receive an additional record, absolutely free!

Do you know how much it would cost to make your own free record?

UP TO **$56,000.00**

and there's even more...

Join **NOW** and receive our publication,

THE TIN EAR describes 500 records that are available, and goes into detail about the ones WE decide YOU are going to get! It's like having a record shop in your home.

Do you realize how much it would cost to have a record shop in your home?

about $100,000...$150,000 in the better part of town.

And if that's not enough . . .

All records must meet our rigid
SPECIFICATIONS
(They must be round and have a hole in the middle.)

Furthermore, they are guaranteed to be brand new and never played. To be sure they have never been played, we play each one three or four times.

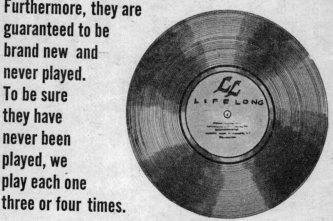

YOU CAN STOP RECEIVING RECORDS ANY TIME YOU WANT!

Just drop us a card and say "Stop sending me records" and we will. However, we will continue to send you bills for the records you don't get until OUR computer says you can STOP paying.

Do you know how much your own computer would cost? About

$1,815,000.

but OURS bills you for free!

And if that don't grab you, how 'bout this . . .

When you join the
LIFELONG
RECORD CLUB

We will send you this free
Deluxe Kit
consisting of a heavy duty
needle and heavy duty cleaning
cloth to help you care for your
records and encourage you
to buy more and more.

Do you know how much it would cost
to buy a factory to make kits like that?
about **$2,000,000!**
How can you afford not to save that much money?
Join Now and Save!

Madison Avenue *Think Tanks* sometimes unknowingly come up with wording that defeats its own purpose . . .

34

Cadillac

THE ROLLS ROYCE OF CARS

BELLE TELEPHONE

We're always
busy... busy...
busy...

THE NEW
BELTUNE
HEARING AID

is really something to shout about!

 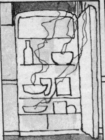 

Well, that's how big corporations could lose by choosing the wrong advertising slogan. But sometimes the small businessman doesn't always help himself either. You'll see what we mean with this assortment of business cards, match books, door signs and like that.

MARRIAGE COUNSELOR

Mrs. Marilyn Hunter

formerly:

Mrs. Marilyn Gaines
Mrs. Marilyn Feldstein
Mrs. Marilyn DeFuccio
Mrs. Marilyn Putnam
Mrs. Marilyn Brenner

Dr. Herman Hermit
PSYCHIATRIST

free balloons with every session

BRIGHT'S BUSINESS SCHOOL

Let us learn you English

courses in:
typeing
speling
all around plannin

ALL HOURS ANSWERING SERVICE

Don't lose business because no one answers your phone.

QU 2 7685

if no answer call back

40

INTERNATIONAL SECURITY CO.

"We Burglar-Proof
Your Premises"

OPEN
WALK-IN

IF NO ONE
IS IN, THE
KEY IS IN
MAILBOX

Antonio's

ITALIAN KITCHEN

"the best food in the city"

OUT TO LUNCH

SAFE HOME
FIRE EXTINGUISHER COMPANY

FIRE SALE
25% OFF
ON ALL SMOKE AND
WATER DAMAGED
EQUIPMENT

ALLIED MEMORY STUDIOS INC.

A fantastic memory
in two months or
your money back!
For more information
mail this coupon to:

CLOSE COVER BEFORE STRIKING

45

He looked at me with those inquiring eyes...I shot back a glance that said:

"Teach me tonight"

...and right then and there he taught me how to make a fire, how to chop wood and all the exciting things that make camping out so much fun!

Dear Reader,

Are you angry? Do you feel like you've been taken? No? Then why were you drooling on the first page, and foaming at the mouth on this one?

Yes, the opening of this chapter was deceptive, but not half as deceptive as book publishers who use:

Sexy, Smutty, Come On Covers

to sell slow moving books.

f'rinstance...

The heat's on with
HOT STUFF

"SALTY!"
"SPICY!"
"PEPPERY!"

Yes, you'll enjoy HOT STUFF with over 500 recipes you can serve piping hot in minutes!

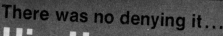

There was no denying it...

His Heart was Mine Forever!

A young woman tells about her feelings after doctors transplanted the heart of an older man...in place of her failing one.

He whispered: "Let's try it once, just for kicks!" ...and now our life is just

ONE FAR-OUT TRIP AFTER ANOTHER

A warm, humorous story about two hippies who actually left Greenwich Village to visit Paterson, N.J., and loved it so much, they went on to visit Nyack, N.Y., Westport, Conn., Pittsburgh, Pa. and other far-out places.

Backseat Tease

and other hair-do tricks a woman can do while traveling by car

53

SHE SAT THERE HALF-NAKED AND SAID:
Teach me everything there is to know about

The Low Life

at first she was
just interested in
hearing about it...
but before she knew it
she was in over her head!

AN EXCITING STORY ABOUT PLANKTON AND
OTHER FORMS OF LOW LIFE IN THE OCEAN

Bikes, Babes & Barbiturates*

*PLUS MANY OTHER SUBJECTS CAN BE FOUND IN THIS VOLUME OF THE NEW KNOW-ALL ENCYCLOPEDIA

Another trick of the advertising trade is to give you the good news on the outside of a package, and the bad news on the inside. That way when you read the label in the store you'll buy it. When you get home and read the bad part, it will be too late, because you had to rip open the package in order to read the bad news. Let's take a closer look at how that gimmick works:

Sounds good, right? Now get it home, and read the instructions INSIDE the box . . .

DIRECTIONS

1. Buy two pounds of ground sirloin steak, brown in olive oil, add minced onions, chopped up fresh green peppers, and garlic.
2. Boil the noodles in bag "A."
3. Add milk to the contents of bag "B" and simmer 2 hours and 40 minutes.
4. Drain the noodles from bag "A," and rinse in 78 degree water. While doing this, keep stirring the simmering ingredients from bag "B" or they will burn and you'll have to start over.
5. Don't let the meat (step one) burn either.
6. Now add meat to bag "B" ingredients.
7. Add melted butter to noodles.
8. Add meat and bag "B" mixture to noodles.
9. Set aside one pint of fresh cream until sour.
10. When cream is thoroughly sour (about 48 hours), re-heat everything else.
11. Now **serve in only one minute**, or the ingredients will coagulate and spoil!

BAG

The Inviting Outside:

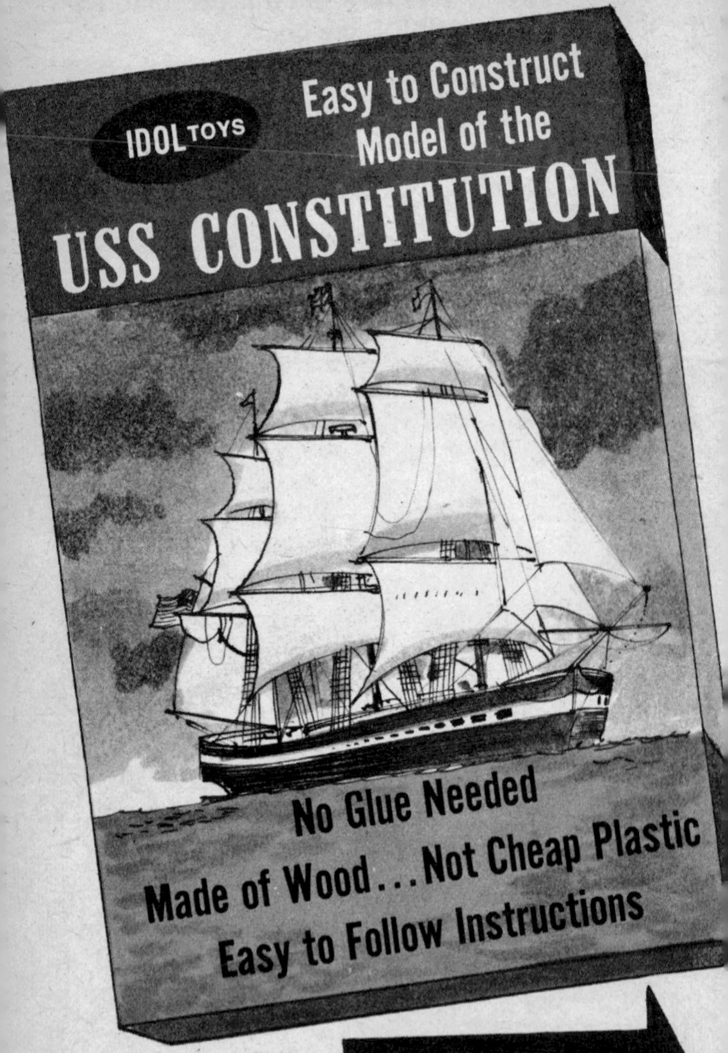

The Bad News Inside

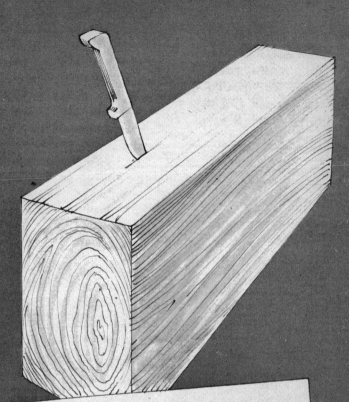

Easy to follow instructions for building this model of the

USS CONSTITUTION

Take the enclosed block of wood, 3 feet long, one foot high and 10 inches thick, and using the knife supplied with this kit, merely cut away every bit of wood that does not look like the cover illustration. Then sandpaper to a smooth finish and paint your model exactly as it appears on the cover.

Another way advertisers use to give you "bad news" or "qualifying statements" is to place an asterisk (∗) next to the big print, which refers you to the real truth in the small print... f'rinstance:

Now Fly to Miami Via ITA Airlines for Only $56 ROUND TRIP*

*Fly any Wednesday during Passover that the plane
is less than 1/8 full, including the crew, and
you must stay in Miami for at least two years,
four months, three weeks and five days and return
on a windy Thursday in Lent on any flight that is
carrying penguins as air freight.

The New **Punto**

COMPLETE PRICE $**1995**[*]

*

Plus federal, state and local taxes, dealer preparation charges, freight and handling, plus certain equipment required by law and certain equipment needed to run the car, like engine, tires and frame...and certain comfort features like seats, doors and windshield...also certain glamour items like roof, floor, bumpers, door handles, etc.

The *Bald One* PIANO

GUARANTEED FOR 5 YEARS *

The five years are: 1944, 1963, 1969, 1973 and 1999. If your piano becomes defective during any one of those five years, return in the original carton, along with a self-addressed prepaid return carton to our factory in Hong Kong. Be sure to include the piano bench and the person or persons who play the piano. Allow two years for return, and keep in mind that a trip to a faraway place like Hong Kong is very bad for a delicate musical instrument like a piano.

TYMIX
WATCHES

Guaranteed Waterproof*

Free Repair Service✳✳

✳As long as case, crown and crystal are intact, and the band doesn't ever get wet...and you don't take it to the beach, swimming pool, tub or shower...and you do not perspire overtly.

✳✳If you meet all the above requirements and conditions, and your watch still fails to function, simply return it in a carton that the post office cannot mishandle (steel is recommended) and just enclose $49.50 for handling charges. There is absolutely no extra charge for the repair service.

65

TABLECLOTHS
Imported
LINEN
$1.00*

*Sold only with
24 imported linen
napkins at $2.50 each

BRAINES
DOG BISQUITS

SAVE UP TO 71¢

See details on coupon inside.

COUPON

This coupon, when mailed to Braines Dog Bisquit Company is worth 2¢, but if you don't mail it at all, you save 8¢ on First Class postage. To really save money, do not sent it to us via AIR MAIL SPECIAL DELIVERY, and you'll save a whopping 71¢

Bird's Foot
FROZEN CARROTS
In Brown Sugar

SAVE UP TO 35¢ WITH ENCLOSED COUPONS

SAVE 10¢
On a Ten Pound Block
of Busy Bee scented
sealing wax

SAVE FIVE CENTS
on Jappy Chocolate
Covered Roaches

8¢ OFF
ON YOUR NEXT PURCHASE
of Chippy Ground Glass
(50 Pound Bag)

SAVE 12¢ ON
DOWN HOME
Aged Watermelon Rinds
in soy sauce

There's an old saying: "Statistics don't lie." That may be true, but when advertisers use statistics, they may not lie, but they sure know how to bend the truth!

...for example, suppose the makers of GLINT Shoe Polish sell only one case of polish in January...then in February, they manage to sell TWO cases. Here's what an ad agency can do with that statistic...

Suppose ten people are asked to try a new brand of coffee and six of them think it's pretty good... In print it might look like this:

THE VOTES ARE IN
and the
MAJORITY
of tasters say
Waxmell House
Coffee is Delicious

Yes, a whopping 60% of everyone we asked agreed, WAXMELL HOUSE is Best! When more than HALF of the experts agree, it must be true!

Get Waxmell House
C O F F E E

73

...and finally, assume there are two really bad brands of margarine on the market...BLEEK-STONE and BLUE HAT...During a whole week, one person buys a package of BLEEKSTONE, and two people each buy a package of BLUE HAT...that's a grand total of three packages of margarine sold in one week for BOTH companies, which is nothing to shout about, right? Well...just give a look at what an ad agency can do with that little old fact...

Blue Hat

MARGARINE
Clobbers Its Competition
By TWO to ONE!

Yes, that's right! Our recent sales charts prove that we've sold twice as much margarine as our nearest competitor.

When that many people buy
BLUE HAT
you know it must be good!

Another gimmick to aid sales is the use of games and premiums...a game might work something like this:

PLAY TIGER GASOLINE'S
WINNER
G A M E

Every time you fill up with TIGER GASO-LINE, you'll receive an envelope with a letter in it . . . just save the letters until you can spell W-I-N-N-E-R and you will have won a jet trip around the world or some other equally exotic place!

FILL UP TODAY!

. . . and here is how that game is probably set up:

- One million envelopes containing the letter "W" are sent all over the U.S.
- Two million envelopes with the letter "I" are sent all over the U.S.
- Three million "N" envelopes are sent all over the U.S.
- Four million envelopes containing the letter "E" are sent all over the U.S.
- **Five** envelopes containing the letter "R" are sent to Red China! (To insure that they don't accidentally fall into the hands of someone who might possibly be playing the game, they are sent third class, and arrive about six months after the contest has expired.)

And then there are those games that really aren't games at all . . . like:

Fill in the missing letters to spell out the name of a well known dance, and you'll WALTZ off with a $50 dance course, absolutely FREE!

W _ _ L _ _ Z

Figure out this brain teaser and you'll be eligible for a grand prize that will have you WALTZing in the aisles!

sorry, but we can't give any hints.

There are also the games, where if you lose, you lose, and if win, you really lose! Here's one now:

Play the COMMEND Hair Tonic
LUCKY PICTURES GAME

Look at the two half photographs below, then check the next page . . . if either or both halves on the next page match those on this page, you're a winner!

Did either or both of your pictures match up? Then look what you've won!

Each matching deluxe black and white picture is yours to keep forever! But to make your prize really worthwhile, so you can show it off to your friends, send for the exclusive heavy-duty balsa wood frames, at only $14.98 each. Mail a check for $20.00 to cover postage, handling, insurance and huge mark-up to:

FRAME ME AGAIN
BOX 7865
Fool, Indiana

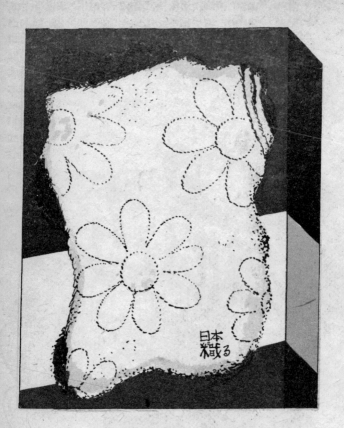
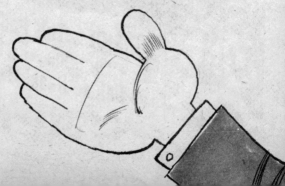

Sure enough, it does contain a beach towel! but if you'll notice, it's on the inside...inside where the detergent should be. So let's see how much room is left for that detergent...It's the giant economy size...3 pounds for $2.70...that's 7.5¢ an ounce. The beach towel has displaced 33 ounces, or $2.47 worth of EXPLODE. The "woven in Japan" label on the towel gives us a clue that it is worth about $1.50 and it cost the company 68¢...which means you just paid $2.47 for a 68¢ beach towel...and since you thought you were cheating the company, you bought six boxes! Since you are such a shrewd shopper, why not rush right out and buy some more copies of this book? They're on sale now for a limited time only for only $2.00 each!

We must admit that most of those premiums are not really all that great...but some premiums really reflect the use of the product. If you don't believe me, just look at all of the neat things you can get with cigarette coupons after you've smoked 5,678 packs...

Complete Home Emergency

OXYGEN KIT!

If you've smoked enough cigarettes to earn all the coupons needed for this prize, you certainly need it, and fast! Your home emergency oxygen is portable, so you can carry it in your car to your office, the golf course, the doctor's office . . . and when that smoking cough strikes, and you gasp for air, it will be right on hand.

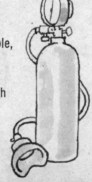

ONLY 5,678 COUPONS

For the Man Who Has Everything!

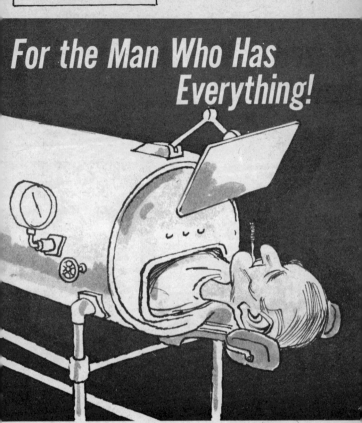

Yes, if you are a man who has everything, including shot-down lungs from smoking too much, now you can have your very own personal iron lung! You'll be one of the few in your neighborhood who will be able to continue smoking right up to that total two lung collapse! And after smoking enough cigarettes to collect the 678,987 coupons needed for this deluxe prize, you deserve it...and God knows you need it! Send for it soon...we know you'll be dying to use it!

Also on the list of advertising gimmicks are Trading Stamps, Gift Coupons and "Cents Off" Deals. Let's check them out one at a time... First, we have "Free" Trading Stamps... are they free? Let's check some store window signs and see.

JOE'S MARKET
Hines Ketchup
39¢
Sorry, no stamps

PIGMY STORES
Hines Ketchup
44¢
and you get FREE
Trading Stamps

FOOD'S FARE
Hines Ketchup
49¢
Extra Special Today
DOUBLE
Trading Stamps

TRIPLE X
XXX
TRADING STAMP

Gift
SELECTIONS

① **27-073 SOLID IRON ANVIL** Ideal for weight watchers or weight lifters .... **59 BOOKS**

② **27-074 SOLID MAHOGANY LUTE CASE** A must for solid mahogany lute players .... **201 BOOKS**

③ **27-075 BARBED WIRE** If you want to protect your prized possessions, like solid iron anvils and mahogany lute cases.

per yd. **15 BOOKS**

④ **072-77 GENUINE IMPORTED ICEBERG** An ideal conversation piece for those dull parties.

4,078 BOOKS, PLUS 5,876 BOOKS FOR SHIPPING

⑤ **270-78 IMPRINTED CHRISTMAS CARDS** Your choice of imprints
. . . check which one you desire:

The Whorrall's . . . John, Beverly,

Harvey and John Jr.

Pam, Chrissy, Spotty and Carl Asmus

Per Dozen .... **60 BOOKS**

⑥ **720-76 SNAZZY AUTOMOBILE DELUXE INITIALS** Bet you've never
seen anything like this in a stamp catalog before! Make your
friends and neighbors green with envy . . . sorry, no "X," "Z,"
"A," "R," "S" or "B" .... **Per initial, 123 BOOKS**

It's easy to tell how big a company is, just by looking at an ad. Here, for example, is a magazine ad run by a company that is very small. Consequently every dollar they spend on their advertising must really push the product . . .

BLAIR ASPIRIN

THE WORLD'S FINEST ASPIRIN

Taken by Doctors, Nurses and People who work in Drugstores!

A product you can take with confidence because Mr. Blair himself fills every bottle!

... and Mrs. Blair puts that tiny wad of cotton into each and every bottle personally!

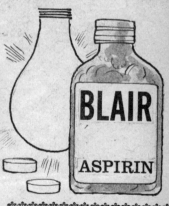

Even little Wally Blair Jr. does his part by screwing the cap on each bottle tightly!

Buy the one, the only, BLAIR Aspirin!... Insist on BLAIR, spelled B-L-A-I-R. Don't disappoint us... your 59¢ bottle of BLAIR Aspirin means everything to us!

QUALITY GUARANTEED
We hold every bottle up to the light to check for broken aspirins!

Remember:
BLAIR! BLAIR! BLAIR!

was commissioned by the makers of Boyer Aspirin.

Boyer Aspirin

without them you may go crazy

Did you ever notice how airlines try to get your business? Since all the airlines use basically the same planes and charge the same fares, they have to come up with a 'gimmick', like telling you that stepping aboard the plane is like stepping into a foreign country, or a tropical paradise, or a fine restaurant. Well, we don't know how far they'll go with these gimmicks, but we'd like to hazard a guess with these...

FUTURE AIRLINE GIMMICKS

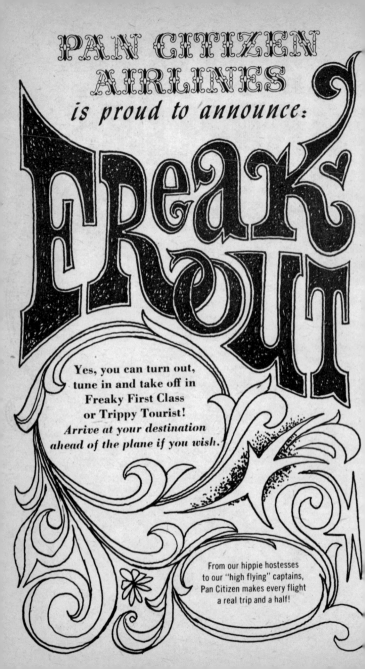

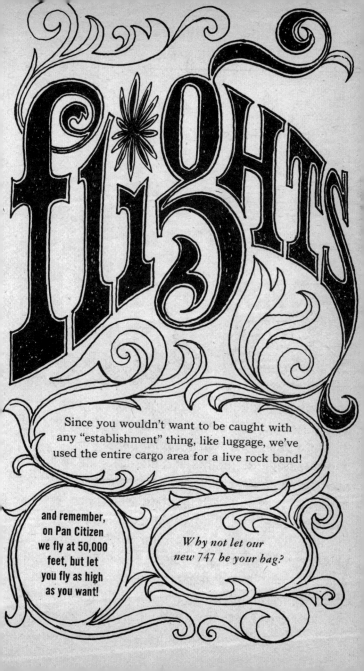

fllGHTS

Since you wouldn't want to be caught with any "establishment" thing, like luggage, we've used the entire cargo area for a live rock band!

and remember, on Pan Citizen we fly at 50,000 feet, but let you fly as high as you want!

Why not let our new 747 be your bag?

Republic Airlines Announces

THE GAMBLER'S SPECIAL

A Brand New Concept in Flights to Las Vegas

Why wait until you actually get to Las Vegas to gamble? Your stewardess will be ready at the loading gate to give you odds on a safe arrival aboard your REPUBLIC JET. And what a jet it is...every seat in first class, and each nine seats in tourist have their own one-armed bandit! Gamble for pennies, nickels, quarters, dollars, your luggage, whatever you want..."The sky's the limit." Wait until you see REPUBLIC'S chorus line of stewardesses...they're the only thing built better than the airplane itself! And talk about drinking...you'll have champagne, imported wine, 14 year old scotch, special rum drinks, plus every kind of hard liquor you can imagine...and that's only the breakfast flights!

Remember, when you think of gambling think of

Republic Airlines

101

Tired of the same old drab stewardesses in Mini-Skirts, Foreign Outfits, Designers Originals and the like?

then step aboard
NORTHERN AIRLINES'
NEW ZOO TRIPS!

Yes, until you step aboard your Northern jet, you won't know
if your stewardess will be dressed as a bunny, a bear or a baboon!
One thing's for sure...no matter what she's dressed like, you'll
still see a lot to remind you that she's a girl!

As soon as you board your zoo flight, you'll thrill to recorded
carousel music, and you'll be given a souvenir balloon. For lunch there's
hot dogs, hamburgers, ice cream...and all the peanuts and popcorn
you want...but for a refreshing change...the animals will be
feeding you!

Yes, Northern Airlines hasn't missed a trick...no human voice will
announce the departure of your jet...instead, a simple cock-a-doodle-do
will tell you to fasten your seatbelts! So next time you fly, make
your reservation with a Northern Elephant Girl...she'll never forget!

Starting Next Week, English Airlines Ltd. Presents

Royal Family Flights

You will be treated like a King or Queen aboard our new British Jetliner, 'The Buckingham'...the only airline that has no seats ... just 152 thrones! As you sit regally on your throne, your humble stewardess will crawl up and down the aisle, catering to your every whim. Instead of movies, a court of in-flight jesters will entertain you or be whipped for your enjoyment.

And talk about food ... you'll have Eggs Rejane; Shrimp Remoulade; Potage Parmentier; Filet of Poisson Amandine; Delmonico Rarebits; Breast of Squab Rotie; Braised Hame A Juif; Beef Wellington; Galantine of Veal; Compote of Fruit Salad; Nesselrode; Camembert, and choice of beverages, which will keep you busy right up until dinner is served. Full orchestra for after dinner dancing, naturally.

Book your next passage on
ENGLISH AIRLINES

You can't miss our jets...they're gold!
Not painted gold, real gold!
Flights every day at IX, XII and VIII

TRANS-LAND AIRLINES
BURLESQUE

presents:
FLIGHTS

On Trans-Land Airlines, the plane isn't the only thing that takes off! As our plane zips, your stewardess strips ... in a rollicking, fun-for-all airborne old-time burlesque show!

Yes, even in perfectly calm weather you'll see 'bumps' aplenty in your Trans-Land Jet, the only jet with the real 'runway' inside the plane. You'll laugh your head off at the shenanigans of your 'baggy-pants' captain and his crew of zanies ... and if you think the sky is blue, wait until you hear the jokes that come over the public address system!

so make your reservations
on **TRANS-LAND** today!
the only airline rated "X"

There is an old advertising expression: "One picture is worth a thousand words." But for some advertisers, one picture could ruin a thousand words. Look at the following ads and then turn the page to see the picture of the product they've carefully omitted. Then you'll understand their advertising logic.

Forget the Old Fashioned
AIR CONDITIONER

Now you can have a **_BREE-ZEE_**

CORDLESS COOLING UNIT
for only $17.95 complete

That's right! No bulky cords or heavy cables . . . No huge electric bill . . . No need to get your landlord's permission . . . No rent hike . . . Special lightweight construction lets you take it in your car, to the office, camping, anywhere you go. Supply is limited, so order today! The complete BREE-ZEE cordless cooling unit costs not $435.00, not $230.00, but only $17.95 plus $2.45 for shipping.

... and here is the actual BREE-ZEE
cordless cooling unit!*

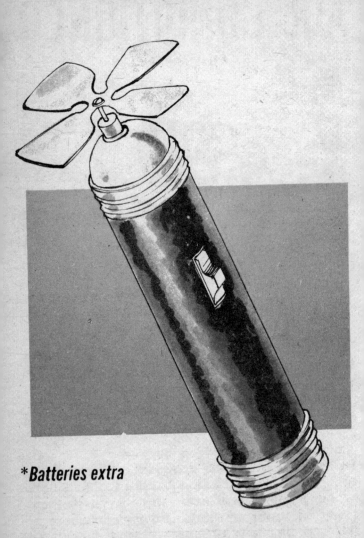

*Batteries extra

ARE YOU PLAGUED BY

A LEAKY BASEMENT?

A LEAKY BOAT?

A LEAKY ROOF?

Then you need a SUPER SUCKER
the modern miracle that makes expensive pumps
OBSOLETE!

The **SUPER SUCKER** lasts for **years** because it has **no moving parts!** Made of a special material that **will not rust!** It's so simple to operate that even a **child** can use it. And for you **boatmen, SUPER SUCKER** works **equally** well in **salt** or **fresh** water.

Your choice of two models: Regular SUPER SUCKER, $6.00,
Heavy Duty SUPER SUCKER, $11.00

Send for yours now, and become a SUPER SUCKER customer!

THE SUPER SUCKER!

Regular

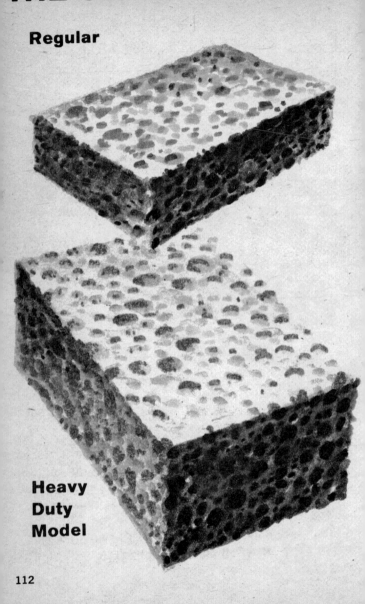

**Heavy
Duty
Model**

Where were YOU when the LIGHTS WENT OUT?

Power blackouts are becoming more and more common. That's why so many businesses, factories, hospitals and homes are turning to their own *auxiliary lighting systems* ... but these systems have always cost hundreds and thousands of dollars. Now the **NEVA DARK MANUFACTURING COMPANY** has devised an auxiliary lighting system for the *home owner* that costs only $19.95 ... a mere *fraction* of the cost of those bigger, more complicated and therefore more troublesome systems. **NEVA DARK** is a *fool-proof,* time tested, **NOISELESS** system that can be used to provide lights in *every room* ... at the same time if you desire! It comes complete with its own "Power Energizer" which you put into use when you *need* it, not before!

Send for your complete **NEVA DARK** Auxiliary Lighting Kit, complete with Power Energizer today! only $19.95

And here it is...the real thing!

Another advertising gimmick very often used is the low priced "look-alike." A second rate manufacturer turns out a second rate product which he designs to look like the original first rate product, but which he sells for 80% less! This ploy is very big in the record industry. Look at these albums and see if you can spot the subtle differences from the originals.

THE SOUND OF MUSIC

takes a real beating from the
PS 86 High School Band!

HELLO DOLLY

A reading of
LETTERS
from
President
JAMES MADISON
to his wife
Dolly Madison

CHITA REVERE   DICK VAN DUKE

. . . explain why birds go south in winter.

MY FAIR LADY

a selection of
hog calls performed
by a lady champion
at the county fair

ON A CLEAR DAY

YOU CAN SEE FOREVER

BUT NOT FOR LONG

A STUDY IN POLLUTION

HAIR

HOW TO
COMB,
CLEAN &
STYLE IT
AS TOLD
BY MISTER
RICHARD

You are about to see an unbelievable tire torture test to prove to you that Badyear Tires can really take it. Our engineers are littering the track with nails, broken glass, rusty spikes and sharp tin can lids to simulate a typical city street.

All set...our test driver starts out slowly...now he's picking up speed...about 40 miles per hour...he's now starting through the bed of nails, broken glass and...

BAM!

...AND HE MADE IT! Not a puncture, not a bit of air lost.... What a test! WHAT a test! And ladies and gentlemen you saw it with your own eyes!

Sure you saw it with your own eyes ... but all you saw with your own eyes was take number 457! What about takes 1 through 456? They ended up on the cutting room floor, or more likely in the Badyear factory's incinerator.

And of course one of the greatest advantages of film is the ability to edit, just to "cut out" a little piece of unwanted action... f'rinstance, look at this short piece of edited film...

And now, let's take a look at another piece of film that has been carefully cut up to protect the sponsor . . .

Mrs. Lashley has taken this brand new white shirt and stained it with mustard, ketchup, ink, blueberry pie and beet juice.... How are you ever going to get that shirt clean, Mrs. Lashley?

With new WHISP... just soak for ten minutes, wash and...

133

Mrs. Lashley has taken this brand new white shirt and stained it with mustard, ketchup, ink, blueberry pie and beet juice....How are you ever going to get that shirt clean, Mrs. Lashley?

With new WHISP...just soak for ten minutes, wash and...

135

then bring in the gray washing machine and the gray kitchen background...and make sure Mrs. Lashley has changed into her "dingy dress" so our test shirt will look that much brighter!

30 MINUTES LATER

...here it is! just like new!

137

139

140

142

There is yet another form of "editing" ... In the desire to have advertising photographs appear more natural, many advertising agencies are actually "going on location" to photograph real people using the real product. Then they can say the picture was not posed, but real. True, but when a photo is not exactly what they want, they do have a little gimmick to fall back on ...

... it's called "cropping," or leaving out the portion of the picture they don't want you to see. Here are a few ads with photographs as they might appear in a magazine, followed by the same photographs before they were "cropped."

148

Nothing completes an evening like *Wine*

No matter what your taste or **budget**, there's
a wine for you.

NATIONAL *Wine* ASSOCIATION

Now Capture all the Fun Sparkle and Tenderness of Your Own Family on Film!

Yes, for years to come you can enjoy their antics in your very own home movies ... Everybody likes to be in the movies, and with Bell & Holler equipment, it's super simple!

When your kids start to yell and howl,

shoot them with **BELL & HOLLER**

For the Man who

For he who dares to take the lead...get away from the beaten path, there's only one...

Dares to be Alone!

Linden

CONTINENTAL

... and here's the true story!

Another dishonest way of advertising is done by "omission." You've seen it many times, most often in movie ads. They take a dreadful review like this:

ETERNAL SPRINGTIME

...a great film for sleeping!

What could have been a very funny film, turned out to be a clinker at yesterday's preview. A really good cast labored in vain to save a perfectly awful plot. The only time the audience was moved was when the words "THE END" flashed on the screen... then they cheered! Director Carl Asmus is about as far from being a professional as one can get. He never has been, and I'm sure never will be Academy Award material. Take my advice, don't go out of your way to see ETERNAL SPRINGTIME.

ETERNAL SPRINGTIME

...a great film for sleeping!

What could have been a very funny film, turned out to be a clinker at yesterday's preview. A really good cast labored in vain to save a perfectly awful plot. The only time the audience was moved was when the words "THE END" flashed on the screen...then they cheered! Director Carl Asmus is about as far from being a professional as one can get. He never has been, and I'm sure never will be Academy Award material. Take my advice, don't go out of your way to see ETERNAL SPRINGTIME.

Eternal Springtime

...a great film!

a very funny film!

a really good cast!

a perfect plot!

the audience was moved...they cheered!

director Carl Asmus is professional!

Academy Award material, I'm sure!

Take my advice, go out of your way to see

ETERNAL SPRINGTIME

Omission is bad enough, but there's a newer and even sneakier advertising technique called "inclusion." It works like this . . . you say something about your particular product that is probably true of all similar products, but by mentioning it, you give the buyer cause for alarm about your competition! Like for example:

Ron's Only

TOMATO
SAUCE

Made with whole Italian
tomatoes and spices

DOES NOT CONTAIN ANY
LINSEED OIL OR SHIRT STARCH

PRULL
SHAMPOO

gets hair extra
clean ... without
drowning roots and
causing baldness

Mr. CHIPPER

CHOCOLATE CHIP
COOKIES

Delicious! Made with only pure
ingredients! And no one has
ever died from eating OUR BRAND!

S&R TRADING STAMPS

Backed with a Special Glue that will NOT give you Cancer of the Tongue!

GOLF
GASOLINE
It's All Gasoline
NO WATER
To Rust Your Tank
NO MOLASSES
To Gum Up Your
Engine

We've talked a lot in this book about truth in advertising. Well, it certainly would be wonderful if that same truth were applied to the want ads companies run. If we're going to have 100% honesty, why not have the want ads reflect much more accurately the type of person and the type of service a company gives its customers . . .for example, here are some samples of what we consider totally honest want ads:

ARE YOU HOSTILE?
Do You Mumble When You Speak?
DO YOU HAVE TROUBLE HEARING?

Then the Metropolitan Phone Company has wonderful opportunities for you. Pleasant surroundings, hundreds of other hostile people; fun times . . . giving wrong numbers, disconnecting long distance calls, etc. Free phone calls . . . charge them to someone else's phone.

UNLIMITED ADVANCEMENT

If you do your job well, you can be a supervisor in 5 years.

If you do your job badly, you can be a supervisor in 3 years.

For an appointment, call QU 2-4567 and call it often, it's usually out of order.

UNEMPLOYED?

If you're reading this ad only to write down company names to give them at the unemployment office, you may be able to turn your "cunning" into a full-time job that is almost better than unemployment! Of course, you'll need some background like the ability to put a tiny item in a huge flimsy paper bag; you must be able to look a customer straight in the face and say "we don't have it" when you know you do, but you don't feel like bending down to get it; and you'll need a bit of math for figuring out how much one item costs when they are priced two for ten cents. But if you can handle that and you have nerve enough to look one hundred customers in the face and say "this register is closed" as you take your third coffee break in half an hour, then forget unemployment and come be almost unemployed with us.

CARRY ON THE
F. W. NILLWORTH
TRADITION
Call us sometime this year.

STILL LOOKING?

You say you can't find your place in modern technology? Then you haven't been looking very hard, which is to your credit. Your future might lie with us if you can meet these qualifications: If you're color blind and find it impossible to match color schemes . . . If you think big nuts fit nicely on little bolts . . . If you can install a defective part with pride, and the words "quality control" are not in your vocabulary, then you can become a part of the team that invented "Factory Recalls." Come to Detroit and join the hustle and bustle of the

AUTO INDUSTRY

Come by train or plane, but not by car if you're serious about showing up on time for an interview.

WE'RE LOOKING

for people who can vanish for 20 minutes at a time!

PEOPLE

who have the knack of taking 15 minutes to walk 10 steps! If you have these rare qualities, then you belong with Howard Johnstone's Restaurants and Roadside Inns. Put your talents to use! We need your type... We keep getting efficient people applying, and sometimes we have to take them in desperation! Don't waste another minute of your time... work for us, and waste the customer's time instead!

HOWARD JOHNSTONE'S

Restaurant & Roadside Inn Employment Offices

If you phone us, let it ring a long time. We take our good old time answering.

HELP WANTED

If you're a man who can tear a beautiful magazine in half . . . destroy a fine work of art . . . smash a delicate vase . . . and shove a 2-foot package into a 1-foot opening, then your future lies with us at the

NATIONAL POST OFFICE SERVICE

We can't tear, fold and mutilate everything ourselves . . . we need help, and you may have just what it takes to do a really bad job. Why not find out?

TELEPHONE US TODAY!

Don't write, we haven't got the time to wait for your letter to be delivered.

GoodOne's
NOODLES

NOODLE LEVEL

This package contains enough noodles to fill up the cellophane window

Sara Dee

BANANA CAKE

DELICIOUS BANANA CAKE IN A CONVENIENT ALUMINUM PAN.

·

SCRUMPTIOUS BANANA ICING STUCK TO AN UNWIELDY CARDBOARD LID.

SIRLOIN STEAK
Lean meat side up,
Fat, Gristle, Moldy
Side, Down.

RiTZy
CRACKERS

This 16 Oz. Box contains:
 8 Oz. of whole crackers
 5½ Oz. of busted up crackers
 2½ Oz. of crumbs

LISTERHYME

This package contains a special shock-absorbing inner liner to keep the 8 oz. bottle from shaking around and breaking in its 16 oz. outer shell.

Pillsberry's
NOT TOO INSTANT
POTATO MIX

SERVES FOUR
PROVIDED THREE AREN'T VERY HUNGRY

Swansong

THIS TV DINNER CONTAINS:

MEAT LOAF
in Tomato Sauce

FRENCH FRIES
in Tomato Sauce

GREEN BEANS
in Tomato Sauce

APPLE SAUCE
in Tomato Sauce and
on the Meat Loaf

CHOCOLATE BROWNIE
in Tomato and Apple Sauce

The above illustration shows a typical dinner using corned beef hash, after it has been cooked per instructions, then worked over by seven professional chefs and two commercial photographers, plus someone with an extremely vivid imagination.

The Turkey

- *Gives you years of "foul" performance*
- *Everything about it says, "Cheap Cheap"*
- *And you should see it "gobble" the gas!*

PRICE... $2,347.98
FULLY DRESSED... $6,876.89

The All New
ELEPHANT

The trunk is in the front . . . and it holds peanuts! It never lets you forget our repair department. Available only in white . . .

Introducing
The **PIG**

Watch it eat the gas . . . Watch it drink the oil . . . Watch it devour the grease!

Buy yourself a new PIG, and you'll know you've got the finest road hog in the world!

and that's not all...

SAVE **75** CENTS
ON A

Zeppelin Ride

Present this coupon to the purser of either
the Hindenburg or the Graf Zeppelin
and receive a 75¢ discount

75¢   75¢   75¢   75¢

THIS COUPON WORTH

FIFTY CENTS
Toward a
GOURMET DINNER

We've made arrangements with one of Europe's
finest restaurants to give you a 50¢ discount.
All you have to do is find out which restaurant
in Europe, and then present this coupon.

---

12 CENTS OFF
STEREOPHONIC
RECORD DEAL

Who's your favorite singer ... Elvis Presley ... or
Enrico Caruso? Well this coupon entitles you to take
12¢ off the price of any stereo record
they've recorded together.

12 CENTS OFF

12 CENTS OFF   12 CENTS OFF